Tim tips it

T0337126

Written by Alma Puts Keren

Illustrated by Amy Lane

Collins

Tim taps it.

Sam sits in.

Tim nips in.

Sam tips it.

Tim dips it.

Sam pats it.

Tim taps it.

Tim did it.

Dad nips in.

Dad tips it.

Dad pins it.

Tim tips it.

14

🐾 After reading 🐾

Letters and Sounds: Phase 2

Word count: 36

Focus phonemes: /s/ /a/ /t/ /p/ /i/ /n/ /m/ /d/

Curriculum links: Expressive arts and design

Early learning goals: Reading: read and understand simple sentences; use phonic knowledge to decode regular words and read them aloud accurately

Developing fluency

- Your child may enjoy hearing you read the book.
- Take turns to read a page aloud. Check your child notices the full stops and pauses before starting a new sentence.

Phonic practice

- Turn to page 9. Point to **did** and ask your child to sound out and blend this word. (d/i/d – **did**)
- On page 10, repeat for **Dad**. Ask your child which letter sounds are different in **did** and **Dad**. (*/i/ in did, /a/ in Dad*). If necessary remind them that the D in **Dad** is a capital letter because it starts the sentence and **Dad** is a name.
- Look at the "I spy sounds" pages (14–15). Point to and sound out the /d/ at the top of page 14, then point to the duck on the wall and say "duck", emphasising the /d/ sound. Ask your child to find other things that start with the /d/ sound. (*Dad, doll, drawings, dolphin, dinosaur, dog, drum, drink, dots, dice*).

Extending vocabulary

- Ask your child if they can mime the following actions:

  dip a brush in paint   pat some paint   tap a pot   tip your hat